Delicious Picture

A SPECIAL MESSAGE TO THE CHILD
WHO IS GOING TO READ THIS BOOK...

Ezme was lucky because her paint was magic...
But, please don't you eat your pictures, because they
will probably make you feel ill. Your pictures are much
better hanging up on the wall, for everyone to see.

The story of Delicious Picture and all
the drawings in this book are original and have
been specially commissioned for Tesco.

Published by
Tesco Stores Limited.
Created by Brilliant Books Ltd
84-86 Regent Street
London W1R 5PA

First published 2000

Text © 2000 Georgia Byng
Illustrations © 2000 Brilliant Books Ltd
Printed by Printer Trento S.r.l., Italy
Reproduction by Colourpath, England

fun to learn

collection

Delicious Picture

Written by
Georgia Byng

Illustrated by
Neal Layton

One day, Ezme painted a picture of a big cake with her magic paints. It was still wet, but it looked so good, she decided to have a taste. Her picture was delicious! Chocolatey! As she swallowed the last little piece, something **very odd** happened...

Ezme found herself standing in a strange house! Everything looked very... different. Ezme was scared. "**Where am I?**" she said. Just then, there was a knock at the door!

A very funny-looking, long-legged lady walked in.

"Hello," she said. "I'm Miss Frilly... Oh my!" she gasped, peering at Ezme. "You're **very peculiar-looking**... Who drew you?"

"Nobody drew me," replied Ezme, crossly. "And I'm NOT peculiar-looking. I'm a human being, just like you."

"A HUMAN BEING!"

shrieked Miss Frilly.
"What are you doing **here**?
This is the Land of Children's
Drawings, my dear!"

Ezme didn't really understand, so Miss Frilly explained. "Every time a child does a picture, it comes to life. But not in their world. It comes here – to the Land of Children's Drawings."

"I was drawn by a little boy called Leo," Miss Frilly said, proudly. "He drew me

a  and

a

and my

"And what *is* life like in the Land of
Children's Drawings?" Ezme asked.
"Well, the Goodlands are lovely. There are
lots of flowers and houses drawn by
children from **all** over your world.
And it's almost always sunny! But recently,
I'm afraid, life hasn't been lovely at all."
Miss Frilly looked sad.

"You see, Ezme, the Badlands have spoiled everything."
"The Badlands? What are the Badlands?" asked Ezme, starting to worry.

"The Badlands are where all children's **bad** drawings go. It's a dangerous place. The drawings there are mean and nasty! You should see what they do! Yesterday some Badlanders got into my house. They ate my sweets and took all my clothes! Now I'm too scared to go home."

"Perhaps I can help!" said Ezme. "Perhaps I could make those nasty drawings better by drawing them in a nice way."

"Don't be silly, Ezme... drawings can't draw!"

"But I'm NOT a drawing," said Ezme. "I'm HUMAN... I'm ME... and I've still got my purple pencilcase. Please let me try!"

Eventually, Miss Frilly agreed and they
set off across some beautiful countryside.
There were horses and sheep and
cows and a **giraffe** in the fields!
And **ten** suns in the sky!

Ezme was just thinking how much fun
the Land of Children's Drawings was,
when all of a sudden, she saw a squiggle
in the air. A drawing was popping up!
Would it be good or would it be bad?

Ezme watched as a shape slowly uncurled.

A pair of

two

and then a

appeared in mid-air.

Soon there was a whole boy.
With a 'POP' he filled with life.
"Oh no!" Miss Frilly cried.
"He hasn't been given a face...
he's a Blankety Blank! I do wish
children would finish their
drawings properly!"

"Look, Miss Frilly," said Ezme. "Let me show you what I can do." Ezme opened her purple pencilcase. With her favourite pen, she gently drew the best  she could on the Blankety Blank. The mouth moved!

"**Yippee!** I'm nearly here," it shouted. "Now all I need are some eyes and a nose."

Ezme set to work and before
she'd even finished properly,
there was a POP! POP! POP!

and the boy leapt up.
"Oh thank you! Thank you.
I'm called Dwoozel.
How do you doozel?"

"See", said Ezme, "I CAN draw here. Now let's get to your house, Miss Frilly, and sort those Badlanders out."

On the way, Miss Frilly pointed to the dark Badland hills. "That's where the Badlanders come from," she said. "And, oh dear! That's my house! But why *is* it dark **there**?"

As they got nearer to her house, Miss Frilly saw exactly why... BADLANDERS! Outside her house were lots of angry scribbles, a fierce growling dog and a boy with measles who was screaming.

The spiteful drawings slowly came closer and closer. "Help!" cried Miss Frilly. Even Dwoozel was scared.

"Wait!"

shouted Ezme. Quickly, she reached again
for her purple pencilcase...

... and she drew a big smile on one of the scribbles.

"Oooh!" it sighed, "I feel all happy inside now. I'm sorry if I frightened you."

Ezme drew and drew until everyone was smiling, she even drew a 🦴 for the dog. Then she took out her rubber and rubbed out all the little boy's measles!

"We're sorry," the Badlanders apologised.
"We promise we'll buy Miss Frilly lots more
sweets and we'll give her back her clothes."
Miss Frilly was so pleased that she asked
everyone to tea. And do you know what?

Ezme drew hundreds of ⬭ and 🍬.
In fact, she drew everything they needed
for a fantastic party.
Then, they all played games and danced...

... until Ezme started to feel really t i r e d.
So she said 'goodbye' to her new friends.
"I promise I'll come back," she said.
Then, she drew a 🚪 just like the one that
led to her bedroom and... stepped through.

The next thing she knew, she was back home,
in her own little room. Ezme zipped up her
purple pencilcase and smiled.

"That was amazing!" she said.